Arabian Nights

Martin Waddell

Illustrated by
Emma Shaw-Smith

•• dingles&company

First published in the United States of America in 2008 by
dingles & company
P.O. Box 508
Sea Girt, New Jersey 08750

First Printing

Website: www.dingles.com
E-mail: info@dingles.com

Library of Congress Catalog Card Number
2007906341

ISBN
978-1-59646-974-7 (library binding)
978-1-59646-975-4 (paperback)

Arabian Nights
Text © Martin Waddell, 2003
This U.S. edition of *Arabian Nights*, originally published in English
in 2007, is published by arrangement with Oxford University Press.

The moral rights of the author have been asserted.
Database right Oxford University Press (maker).

Printed in China

Contents

Aladdin and the Wonderful Lamp

The Youngest-of-All

Aladdin and the Wonderful Lamp

Chapter 1

An Evil Magician

There once was a lazy boy named
Aladdin. He did nothing but whistle
all day long and grin at the girls.

"You'll come to no good!" warned
his mother.

"Fate will look after me!"
smiled Aladdin.

One day, an evil magician came to
their village. He was searching for
someone he knew would be there.

How did he know? He was a
magician. It was his *business* to know
things like that.

He saw Aladdin and smiled to himself.

"Read the name that is scratched on my ring!" he commanded Aladdin.

The name scratched on the ring was

"Why, sir, that's my name!" gasped Aladdin.

"Fate has led me to you," said the evil Magician. "Take me to your father!"

"My mother is a widow," Aladdin replied.

The Magician saw his chance.
He could pretend to be Aladdin's
long lost uncle.

"You tell me that my poor brother
is dead, Nephew!" he said, cunningly.
"Take me to your mother, at once."

A puzzled Aladdin led the uncle-he-
had-never-heard-of to his mother.

"My husband didn't tell me that he
had a brother," said the widow.

"Old quarrels die hard!" sighed the Magician. "Now how can I help you and my dear nephew, Aladdin?"

"If you could find work for my son, I'd be most grateful," the widow replied.

"I'll do what I can!" smiled the evil Magician.

Everything was working out just as he had planned.

Chapter 2

The Treasure Cave

The next morning, the evil Magician led Aladdin away from the village to a place in the hills. There he lit a fire and tossed a red powder onto the flames.

The fire blazed. A great pillar of smoke rose from it, and the earth cracked and broke.

When the smoke cleared, Aladdin was staring down into the mouth of a cave.

"Here's some work especially for you, *Nephew!*" smiled the Magician. "In that cave, there's a door. You must open it and go in!"

"You do it! You're bigger than I am!" said lazy Aladdin.

"Alas! I can't do it," the evil Magician replied. "A treasure lies there, meant for you, and you only."

"What if there is danger?" Aladdin asked.

"Take the ring with your name
scratched on it," said the Magician.
"It will keep you safe from all danger."

Aladdin slipped the ring on. Then
he touched the door, and it opened
before him.

Aladdin climbed down into the cave.

He found himself in a beautiful room filled with diamonds and jewels and pearls and strange stones that glowed like the moon.

"I've found my treasure, Uncle!" he called to the Magician. "You must have your share for bringing me here."

"There's an old lamp down there that I'd like," the evil Magician called back.

"That's not much to ask for," thought Aladdin, and he brought up some jewels instead.

"I don't want this old stuff. Fetch me the lamp!" barked the Magician.

"Fetch it yourself!" thought Aladdin. He didn't like being barked at. But he went back for the lamp. And he found it. It didn't look much of a lamp.

He thought he'd look in the next room. One room led to another, then on and then on. Each room was filled with a treasure ... gold coins or jewels or silks.

"Bring me my lamp, you young fool!"
the Magician shrieked down the
stairs, growing angry.

Aladdin stayed where he was. He
didn't like being called a young fool.

"Come here with that lamp, you
rotten dog!" bawled the Magician,
dancing with rage. "If you think you
can steal it … you can't. I'll slit you in
two when I catch you!"

"An uncle would never say that!" thought Aladdin. *"He lied to me ... all he wants is this lamp!"*

"I WANT MY LAMP, NOW!" the evil Magician roared, tearing his hair.

His screams and curses echoed down from above ... but Aladdin sat very still, staring at the lamp. It didn't look special. It was just a dirty old lamp.

"There must be something wonderful about this lamp," Aladdin thought to himself.

At last, the evil Magician gave up.

"You'll never escape from the cave!"
he yelled to Aladdin. "You can die
down there, for all I care!"

Then the evil Magician sealed the
mouth of the cave, with his magic.

Aladdin was trapped underground,
alone in the dark.

Chapter 3

A Small Cloud of Smoke

Aladdin was filled with despair.
But then he remembered his ring.
He touched it and …

A small blue cloud of smoke swirled
up, from inside the ring. It floated in
front of Aladdin and spoke to him!

"I serve only you! Where can I take
you, Master?" it said, with a shimmer.

"Take me home!" said Aladdin.
FLASH!

He was back in his own house
with the ring and the lamp. And his
pockets were full of the treasure he'd
found in the cave. Aladdin gave most
of it to his mother, but he held
on to the lamp.

"The lamp might be magic as well," thought Aladdin.

He made a wish. Nothing happened.

"Maybe the lamp will shine up!" he thought.

Then he polished it with a rag and ...

Chapter 4

The Genie of the Lamp

WOOOOOOSH! A cloud of smoke blew out of the lamp, filling the room. A huge genie appeared from the smoke and bowed to the boy.

"I serve the Lamp!" said the genie. "You have only to ask! Whatever you wish for, will be!"

"I ... I'd like a good house for my mother!" Aladdin said, his eyes popping out of his head.

More smoke … and the fine
house appeared.

"The next wish is for me!"
said Aladdin.

He wished for fine food and good
wine, and he feasted all day with
his friends.

He wished for riches, and gold
coins covered the floor.

He wished for a palace to live in ... and there it was, with a glittering roof and a garden with peacocks and roses, and bright pools to bathe in.

He wished for a wife ... and the genie brought him the King's beautiful daughter. She fell in love with him at once and they were married. That made Aladdin a prince!

Chapter 5

The Magician's Revenge

Not every boy from a poor village becomes son-in-law to the King. And of course, people wondered how Aladdin had gotten his riches.

People wondered ... and so did the King.

"This must be the work of a magician," said the King's adviser, the Wazir. "No good can come from it."

"It looks good to me!" replied the
King, who was admiring the presents
Aladdin had brought him.

There were camels and carpets
and jewels and piles of juicy peaches
and apricots and figs and many
strange and wonderful fruits.

"Beware of Aladdin!" warned the Wazir.

"You beware!" said the King,
munching a peach.

Aladdin's story spread through the country, as such stories do.

One day, the evil Magician heard it. He guessed what had happened!

"What Aladdin has, should be mine!" swore the Magician.

And he disguised himself as a man who sold lamps in the street.

"New lamps for old!" cried the evil
Magician, as he walked in front of
Aladdin's palace.

The Princess's maid heard his cry,
and she told the Princess.

"The Master's old lamp is a disgrace
to your beautiful palace. Why don't
we swap it for a shiny, bright lamp
that is new?"

"You're right!" laughed the Princess. "I'll be glad to get rid of that nasty old lamp."

And they swapped Aladdin's magic lamp for a new one. If Aladdin had been there, he would have stopped it. But Aladdin wasn't there. He was with the King, next door.

"The lamp is mine now!" the Magician chortled as he grabbed it.

The next thing they knew –
WOOOOSH! A cloud of smoke. And the
Princess and the palace were swirling
high in the sky, with the evil Magician.

The Magician had wished them
away to his own country, far, far away
from Aladdin.

Chapter 6

An Angry King!

"Where's your palace gone? Where's my daughter?" the King roared at Aladdin, as they looked out of the window at the place where Aladdin's palace had been.

"I told you to beware of Aladdin!" crowed the Wazir. "Cut off his head!"

"Wait!" Aladdin said to the King. "If you cut off my head, you will never see your daughter again. Give me forty days, and I'll find her!"

"Just see that you do. Or you'll die!" said the King.

Aladdin searched everywhere for his wife. But he couldn't find her. Then he remembered that he still had his ring.

He touched it and the small, blue cloud puffed out again.

"Bring my wife back!" Aladdin told the cloud.

"My magic only works with you," the small, blue cloud replied. "I can't bring her to you."

"Then bring *me* to *her*," Aladdin said, thinking fast.

FLASH!

And Aladdin was with his wife, in the palace.

Aladdin hid quickly, so that the Magician wouldn't see him.

When the Magician left the room for a moment, Aladdin came out of his hiding place.

Chapter 7

The Return of the Genie!

"Slip this powder in his drink at supper," Aladdin told his wife. "It will make him fall asleep. I'll find my lamp while he's snoring."

And that's what she did.

Aladdin found his lamp and rubbed it with his sleeve.

WOOOOOSH! The genie appeared, bowing low.

"I serve the Lamp!" the genie began. "Whatever you –"

"Take us back to the King!" Aladdin broke in. "When you've done that, you can deal with that evil Magician!"

The Princess was saved, and so was Aladdin.

No one ever knew what became of the evil Magician, except the genie. No one wanted to know.

Time passed, and the King and his Wazir died of old age.

Aladdin came to the throne, and he was King for many years.

Fate had looked after him, as he knew it would.

Fate – and a wonderful lamp.

The Youngest-of-All

Chapter 1

Two Jealous Sisters

There once was a poor merchant who had three daughters.

The two elder girls were both tall and lovely to look at, but the Youngest-of-all was more beautiful still.

The hair hanging down to her waist was shiny as satin and black as the night. Her eyes shone like stars, and she danced on the daintiest feet in the world.

No one noticed her two sisters, when she was in the room. This didn't please them at all.

They envied the Youngest-of-all. And their envy soon turned to hatred.

"That little toadstool!" they told each other. "Why does everyone love her so?"

Of course they knew why, and it hurt.

Chapter 2

The Magic Flowerpot

The Youngest-of-all was a good-natured girl. She did all she could to be loved.

One day she bought a little flowerpot in the market. She thought it would please her two sisters.

But her sisters weren't pleased!

"Who needs such a plain little pot? You've wasted our poor father's money on nothing!" they told her.

"My little flowerpot," sighed the Youngest-of-all, when they'd gone. "I wish something lovely grew in you."

Before she could blink, a little rosebud popped up through the earth in the pot, tiny and perfect, and red as a ruby.

The Youngest-of-all was amazed, and she called for her sisters.

"Who needs a grubby rosebud like
that?" cried her sisters.

Then they pretended to sneeze and
to choke.

"It's making us ill!" they told the
Youngest-of-all. "Get it out of our house!"

The Youngest-of-all carried the rose
in the pot to her own room.

"My little flowerpot," she sighed.
"I wish something would happen to
please my two sisters."

There was a C-R-A-C-K, and the mirror beside her bed splintered.

The two sisters came running.

"Your mirror is cracked! Now you can't see your stupid face!" they told the Youngest-of-all. And they went away feeling very pleased.

Chapter 3

More Magic

The Youngest-of-all took great care of the pot after that. She kept it safe, and she watered the rosebud that grew in it.

She knew it was no ordinary pot, but a pot that could work magic for her.

"My little flowerpot," she would say. She'd wish ... and whatever she wished for, just happened.

She wished for good wine they
could drink with their supper.
And good wine came.

"Euugh!" gurgled her sisters.
"We can't drink such sour stuff."

She wished for gold combs they
could put in their hair.

"Not our style!" said her two sisters.
They stamped on the gold combs
and broke them into pieces.

She wished for rich perfumes for her sisters.

"Pooh!" said the sisters. They walked around holding their noses.

After that, the Youngest-of-all kept her secret.

Whatever she wished for – fine silks, or diamonds, rubies or pearls, or beautiful books – all vanished completely when her two sisters came into the room. So maybe, the little flowerpot understood.

Chapter 4

The Ball

One day, the King gave a great ball. Everyone was invited, even the sisters.

"We'll need new clothes for the ball!" the two sisters said.

"So will I!" said the Youngest-of-all.

"You're too ugly to go!" the sisters told her. "We can't waste our father's money on new clothes for *you*. You can stay at home and look after the house."

"Is that so?" thought the Youngest-of-all.

The two sisters went to the ball in their new clothes. They danced all night. One of them winked at the Prince, but he didn't take any notice.

He had eyes for no one but a sweet young girl who'd slipped into the ball after everyone else.

She wore beautiful clothes and fine slippers. Jewels shone on her dress, her anklets glittered with diamonds, and her bangles were gold. Her small feet were so neat that she swirled like a feather.

"Who can she be?" everyone asked. "So small ... yet so sweet."

"It can't be *her*!" muttered the envious sisters.

It *couldn't* be. Could it?

"Where could *she* get such beautiful clothes?" they asked each other.

"It must be some rich princess who looks a bit like our ugly young sister," they decided at last.

The Youngest-of-all slipped away before the last dance, so she'd be home before her sisters. Then no one would know that she had been to the ball.

She hurried away from the palace, but she tripped as she ran, and something shiny fell from her ankle.

It was a diamond anklet, so tiny that only a girl with the daintiest feet in the world could wear it.

Chapter 5

The Tiny Anklet

Of course, the Prince found the tiny
anklet the next morning.

"It belongs to that beautiful young
Princess I danced with last night!"
he told the King.

But no one knew who the girl was.

"I'll marry the Princess this anklet
was made for!" the Prince told the King.

49

The Prince and his men searched
everywhere, but they couldn't find
the Princess.

Then they came to the three
sisters' house.

"No king's daughter would live *here!*"
the Prince's men said, scornfully.
But the Prince wouldn't listen.

The two envious sisters tried on
the anklet. But it scarcely passed
over their toes.

Then the Youngest-of-all raised her
tiny foot and the anklet slipped on.

It fitted perfectly.

That was the
end of the search.

"This is *my* Princess!" the Prince told
everyone. "I don't care if her father
isn't a king!"

The King and the Queen didn't think
much of that ... until they met the girl.
Then, like everyone else, they fell under
her spell.

"How did you do it?" the two sisters asked her. "How did you get those fine clothes and jewels to go to the ball?"

The Youngest-of-all shared her secret with them.

She gave them her little flowerpot and the tiny rosebud that grew in it.

"It worked for me," she told them. "I know it will work for you, too."

Chapter 6

The Sisters' Plan

The sisters wished to be rich ... and gold coins tinkled all over the floor.

They wished for servants ... and a hundred young men and young women bowed at their door.

They wished for a feast ... and their table groaned under the weight of the food.

Soon, they had all they could wish for, and more.

The sisters should have loved their young sister for changing their lives. But it didn't work out quite like that.

They both stood and looked at the pot.

"We're just as good looking as she is," they told each other.

"Much better looking – and bigger!" they said to themselves.

"If she wasn't around, the Prince would choose one of *us* in her place!" they decided.

"If only she were a bird, who would fly away!" one of them said. Then they stopped and looked at the little flowerpot, and they grinned at each other.

"Turn her into a blackbird because of her hair?" said one.

"A blackbird might peck us!" the other replied.

"Make her a gentle dove!" they decided.

They grabbed hold of the little flowerpot and they wished.

Out of the pot came seven pins studded with diamonds.

"Pins?" the sisters said to each other. "What use are pins?"

Then they thought of their sister's shiny black hair flowing down to her waist. They ran to the Youngest-of-all.

"We love you *so* much, *dear* little sister," they said. "Let us comb your beautiful hair and use these lovely pins to hold it in place."

The Youngest-of-all kissed her sisters. She let them comb her long hair, shiny and satin and black as the night.

As they combed, they slipped the pins into her beautiful hair.

As the last pin went in, the room seemed to shiver and shake ... and the Youngest-of-all vanished.

A little dove fluttered where she had been. The two sisters tried to capture her. But she escaped and flew away through the open window.

Chapter 7

The Prince and the Dove

The two sisters pretended to help in the hunt for the Youngest-of-all. They searched high and low, weeping false tears.

"Let us comfort you," they told the Prince. "We miss her too. We know what you must be feeling."

The Prince had no time for the sisters. He'd lost his Princess, and he was heartbroken.

The Prince grew pale and thin. He stayed in his room and never spoke. He would let no one near him, except a little dove who came each morning at dawn, and each night at twilight.

She cooed softly outside his window, as though she was trying to comfort him.

One day, he opened his window, and the dove flew in and perched on his hand. She nestled her head against him.

"My little dove," sighed the Prince. He felt her tiny heart beat as he stroked her feathers.

Something hard pricked his hand, as he stroked.

It was a pin, with a diamond set in it.

"Poor little dove," said the Prince. "I think this hurts you. Let me pull it out."

Gently, he pulled the pin out, and then he found another.

So it went on, until he pulled the seventh pin out of her feathers. The dove cooed in delight. The room seemed to shiver and shake. A sweet-scented mist swirled around the Prince ...

... and the Youngest-of-all stood before him.

Of course, they were married at once.

Whatever happened to the
two sisters?

They were afraid that the
Youngest-of-all would tell the Prince
what they had done. So they fled …
and were never heard of again.

When her wedding night came, the
Youngest-of-all had a gift for her Prince.

"What's this?" the Prince smiled.

"It's my rosebud, and my little
flowerpot," said the Youngest-of-all.

And the little rosebud blossomed
into a rose.

About the author

I don't know much about the
background of these stories. What I do
know is… they are good stories. Things
happen, and the things that happen
change the people they happen to.

The lazy way to spoil a story is to
put "Then I woke up. It was all a
dream!" Nothing has *changed*, nothing
has *happened!*

If you want to write a good story,
something funny or exciting or
interesting has to happen in it.